Dog Diaries

by Clare Lawrence
Illustrated by David Shephard

Titles in Ignite

Alien Sports TV	Jonny Zucker
Monster Diner	Danny Pearson
Team Games	Melanie Joyce
Mutant Baby Werewolf	Richard Taylor
Rocket Dog	Lynda Gore
The Old Lift	Alison Hawes
Spiders from Space	Stan Cullimore
Gone Viral	Mike Gould
The Ghost Train	Roger Hurn
Dog Diaries	Clare Lawrence

Badger Publishing Limited
Suite G08, Stevenage,
Hertfordshire SG1 2DX
Telephone: 01438 791037   Fax: 01438 791036
www.badgerlearning.co.uk

Dog Diaries ISBN 978-1-84926-967-4

Text © Clare Lawrence 2012
Complete work © Badger Publishing Limited 2012

All rights reserved. No part of this publication may be reproduced, stored in any form or by any means mechanical, electronic, recording or otherwise without the prior permission of the publisher.

The right of Clare Lawrence to be identified as author of this Work has been asserted by her in accordance with the Copyright, Designs and Patents Act 1988.

Publisher: Susan Ross
Senior Editor: Danny Pearson
Designer: Fiona Grant
Illustrator: David Shephard

Dog Diaries

Contents

Chapter 1	**Puppy**	5
Chapter 2	**Hard work**	9
Chapter 3	**Nightmare!**	15
Chapter 4	**Fireworks**	20
Chapter 5	**Wonderful day**	26
Hearing dogs		30
Questions		32

Vocabulary:

believe   bargain
recipient   injection
disaster   embarrassing

Main characters:

Sam

Kip

Chapter 1

Puppy

April 8th
I can't believe it. We're getting a puppy!

I've struck a deal with Mum. If I work harder at school, stop winding up Ricky and promise to keep my room in order, we're going to be able to socialise a hearing dog puppy!

It was in the paper that the charity needs people to look after the pups until they are old enough to train. I never thought Mum would say yes.

Linda, the area trainer, came round today. She was pleased that our garden has a good fence and that Mum is at home all day.

I really, really can't wait! I am going to keep this diary so I don't forget a thing.

April 28th

Linda called. We are going to be looking after a black spaniel pup called Kip! He is six weeks old now and will come to us at eight weeks. That's in just TWO WEEKS' TIME!

May 14th

Kip comes today! I tried to get out of school so I could be here, but I didn't give Mum too much grief when she said no.

I'm trying really hard to keep my end of the bargain. Kip will be there when I get home...

Later

He's here. He is SO cute! He is black with a white patch on his chest. He has long ears and the softest coat.

He has a sweet face and big brown eyes... and he is SO SMALL!

Chapter 2

Hard work

May 15th

Kip slept on the landing just outside my room in his crate. He only whined a bit in the night.

At six o'clock he woke up and I took him down to go out. I used to hear Mum get up in the night with Ricky.

Now I know what it's like. I can see this is going to be hard work...!

May 22nd

Took Kip to the vet for his injection. He can go out from next week. I've taught him to sit for a treat and now I'm starting on 'Down'.

He's dead smart.

May 30th

Kip goes out for the first time today. Mum says we should let him off the lead, but what if he runs off and disappears?

Linda told us that young puppies stay close to you, but what if something frightens him and he freaks out?

Later

I didn't want Mum to let Kip off the lead and I walked off when she said she was going to.

I didn't want to be there when disaster struck! But Linda was right. Kip stayed right beside us when he was off the lead.

Mum called me over and said it was OK. I walked with Mum and Kip walked really near us.

Every time a dog came near, he ran back to us until he was sure it was friendly.

June 7th

Today we took Kip into the library to get used to meeting people.

Everyone made a real fuss of him – and guess who was there? You guessed it: Matt!

He came over and rubbed Kip's ears (lucky Kip!). I had to keep telling people that Kip isn't ours. He is a hearing dog puppy and we will only have him for nine months or so.

They all asked the same thing, "How can you give him up?" I wish they wouldn't ask that. I don't know how I'm going to say goodbye either.

Chapter 3

Nightmare!

June 11th

Nightmare! We took Kip to the shopping centre this morning.

He was being calm and not jumping up too much when he met people, but then he peed on the floor!

I was so ashamed and we had to say sorry like mad.

To make it worse, Matt came past just as the manager was clearing it up. Talk about embarrassing!

The manager was quite nice about it really but he called it a "dirtying event".

Now, when my baby cousin's nappy needs changing, Mum puts on a posh voice and calls it that and we crack up.

July 23rd

I hate him! He's a horrible dog and I wish we'd never got him. He chewed my phone! It's ruined! I can't text or phone anyone and now no one can get in touch with me all holiday.

I won't see anyone and it will be all his fault!

Later

I've said sorry to Kip. I know it wasn't his fault, really. I shouldn't have left my phone on the floor.

Mum says that if I wash the car, inside and out, and cut the grass and clean the downstairs windows, she'll take me to get a new phone.

It'll only be a rubbish, cheap one, but at least I can save the SIM and keep my old number.

August 22nd
Went to see the new film with Carys and Harjot, and guess who was there? Even better, he says he wants to do a project on charity dogs for his community paper next year.

He'll have to come round and ask me about Kip and take some pictures. Oh thank you, thank you Kip – I love you!

September 9th
Back to school this week and already it is getting dark earlier. Soon we won't be able to walk Kip after school, so I'll do lots of training with him instead. It's good for him to use his brain, and it helps to tire him out.

Chapter 4

Fireworks

November 5th
Matt is coming round after school to do his charity dog project work. I'm really nervous!

Later
Brilliant afternoon! Matt made a real fuss of Kip and asked loads of questions. Then he said that a group of them are going to the fireworks in town later.

I've asked Mum and she says I can go. She's got to stay here to look after Kip in case he's frightened.

I was really worried she'd say I had to take Ricky, or something, but she didn't. No Mum, no puppy, no younger brother. Yes!

Later still
I'll never forget this evening. I've never been so happy!

November 9th

Today Kip is having his big assessment.

If he fails, then Linda says that he may not be the right dog for a deaf person. Then he will need to be found a new home with a family on the re-homing waiting list.

Mum has told me we are not allowed to keep him.

Perhaps that's just as well, or it would be just too tempting to teach him to do something bad.

Later

He passed! Linda says he's a really great dog (she's right) and will be ready to go into training in about eight weeks' time.

I know I should be proud, and I am, but it will just be so hard to say goodbye.

November 26th

Kip goes next Thursday. Linda is coming to collect him. I begged and begged Mum to let me stay at home, but she says I have to go to school.

I got in a sulk, but Mum didn't get cross. She just made me a cup of tea.

December 3rd

Kip goes tomorrow. I've been crying. I know it is silly. I always knew he wasn't really ours, but it is so difficult.

I love him so much.

Later

I have brought Kip up to bed with me. He is on the floor by the bed now, fast asleep. I think Mum heard me, but she didn't say anything. I know she is going to miss Kip too.

Even Ricky will miss Kip.

Kip – we're all really proud of you. We have been so lucky to share your growing up and see you turn from a little pup into the fine young dog you are now. I know you will make a huge difference to someone's life. I'm proud of you, Kip. I'll never forget you.

Chapter 5
Wonderful day

December 4th

He's gone. It is horrible. Mum's eyes are red and I know she's been crying too.

She says we're going to get a pizza and watch a film together tonight to cheer ourselves up.

She treats me more like another adult now. I think looking after Kip has helped me to grow up a bit.

I owe him so much... and I miss him so much.

Later

Matt texted to see if I'm OK.
Just made me cry even more.

March 13th

A wonderful day! We went to the training centre to see Kip.

He can alert to an alarm clock and a kitchen timer. He is so clever!
He looks really well and happy, but it is like he has grown up and moved on.

He will go to his recipient soon, and then he will be that person's dog... and that person's ears. I know what a great job these dogs do for people who are deaf.

I felt like dancing with pride today, and I thought the day just couldn't get any better.

But it could! On the way home, Mum and I had a long talk.

Guess what? Our names are on the list for our next pup!

By the holidays, we should have another little puppy to house-train and clear up after, to play with and teach. I'll never forget Kip, but I understand now.

He is just the first. I wonder what our next hearing dog pup will be called…

Hearing dogs

Hearing Dogs for Deaf People is a charity which trains dogs to alert deaf people to important sounds and danger signals.

These are sounds, such as the alarm clock, doorbell, baby monitor, telephone or mobile phone, text alert or smoke alarm.

There are over 750 working hearing dogs in the UK today.

Hearing dogs alert by touching with a paw or their nose to gain attention, then leading to the sound.

For danger signals, such as the smoke alarm, the hearing dog will alert in the same way but will then lie down to show danger.

Hearing dogs spend the first nine to twelve months with a volunteer socialiser. They learn basic obedience and to be polite and calm when they meet strangers and other dogs.

Hearing dog puppies are encouraged to go into places where dogs are not normally allowed.

They need to get used to shops, lifts and public transport for when they are working dogs.

The dogs then go on to soundwork training and are matched with a recipient.

They become that persons 'ears', and also give confidence and companionship.

Support from the charity continues throughout the dog's working life.

Questions

What date does the story begin?

What was the name of the area trainer?

What day did Kip meet Sam?

Who broke Sam's phone?

Where did Sam go on November 5th?

What kind of dog do you think Sam will be given to look after next?